In loving memory of my mother, Anne Davidson Halliday.
"Gently, gently, gentleness . . ." (Louis MacNeice, "Autobiography")

First published in 2020 by Page Street Kids,
an imprint of Page Street Publishing Co.
27 Congress Street, Suite 105
Salem, MA 01970
www.pagestreetpublishing.com

Distributed by Macmillan, sales in Canada by The Canadian Manda Group

19 20 21 22 23 CCO 5 4 3 2 1

ISBN-13: 978-1-62414-999-3
ISBN-10: 1-62414-999-5

CIP data for this book is available from the Library of Congress.

This book was typeset in Spencer.
The illustrations were done in traditional and digital mixed media.

Printed and bound in Shenzhen, Guangdong, China

Page Street Publishing uses only materials from suppliers who are committed
to responsible and sustainable forest management.

Page Street Publishing protects our planet by donating to nonprofits like The Trustees,
which focuses on local land conservation.

Numenia and the Hurricane

Inspired by a True Migration Story

Fiona Halliday

PAGE
STREET
KIDS

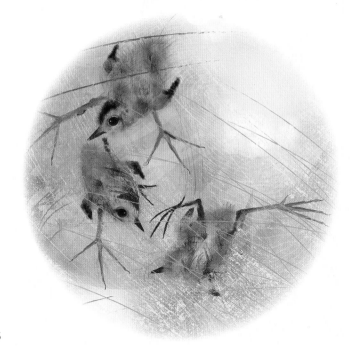

Three sisters born
By arctic shore
On bare, cold rock
As spring winds roar.

Bandit-eyed,
They slip unseen
Through beckoning moors
Of tangled green.

Hunting bugs in
Thawing creeks.
Spearing, gobbling,
Growing beaks.

Five weeks old,
They've reached the sky!
"Curlee, curlee,
Curloo," they cry.

Suddenly,
It's equinox.
Autumn calls
Its feathered flocks.

Thousands gather
On the moor,
Babbling, jostling,
But unsure . . .

'Til wise old goose
Shows them the way,
Surging out of
Hudson Bay.

Three sisters rise
And seek the height,
Guided by the
North Star's light.

But from the skies
A great stampede!
Ten thousand hissing
Raindrops freed!

One ripped away!
She claws the air,
Blinded by the
Lightning glare!

Down she swoops,
Her feathers flail.
A tiny *peeeep* . . .
A screeching wail!

Escape, escape
The awful shriek!
Faltering,
She's wet and weak.

Askew upon
A windowsill:
A dripping ghost
With trembling bill.

A moon face in
A glowing pane.
Fingers reaching
Through the rain.

In restless dreams,
She's one of three:
Three sisters in a
Tangled tree.

She lifts her eyes,
She longs for flight,
Surging into
Dawn's red light.

On stronger wing
She battles on.
Searching, seeking,
She is drawn.

With storm-tossed birds
Like ragged ghosts,
She hugs the lines
Of battered coasts.

She's half the weight
She was before;
A clutch of hope
And nothing more.

But from the sigh of
Distant waves,
Echo sweet and
Haunting staves!

"Curlee, curlee,
Curloo," they ring.
Through sundered skies
Her feathers sing!

In crumbled rainbows
Spindrift spun,
She's molten gold
In sinking sun.

Wild trees wade
The foaming tide.
Egrets hiss,
Fish glint and glide.

Around her, roots
Snatch, entrap!
Paw her, claw her,
Croak and flap!

Then, weary-winged,
She sinks her toes
In rippling warmth;
It's home, she knows.

And cloaked
In dancing fireflies,
Singing softly,
Two shapes rise!

Here, where moon
And shadows meet,
Three joyful sisters
Softly greet.

And so their bond
Is forged anew . . .
"Curlee, curlee,
Curloo."

The True Story That Inspired This Book

The name "Numenia" comes from *Numenius phaeopus*, the Latin name for whimbrels, a type of migratory shorebird. When I first saw a whimbrel on the Shetland Islands in Scotland, I was immediately fascinated. Despite my love of birds, I knew very little about whimbrels. Then I read about Hope.

Hope was a whimbrel that scientists from the Center for Conservation Biology at the College of William and Mary tracked between 2009 and 2012. Every year as Hope flew her migration route, they gathered information through a tiny solar-powered satellite transmitter that she wore like a backpack.

In 2011, the scientists witnessed something astonishing! As Hope set off on her annual migration from Canada's Northwest Territories to the US Virgin Islands, she ran into Tropical Storm Gert off the coast of Nova Scotia. She battled through raging headwinds for twenty-seven hours nonstop, going an average of nine miles per hour! Would this little bird, with nothing to fuel her but a belly full of tundra berries, make it? She must have been *exhausted*.

Not only did she survive the storm, but afterward, she used its headwinds to hurl herself back toward Cape Cod. Days later she arrived in St. Croix, where she spent the winter feeding on fiddler crabs, before her long migration back to Canada in the spring.

Hurricanes can be devastating for migratory birds like Hope and Numenia. Blown hundreds or thousands of miles off course, they are weakened and exposed to predators. Hurricanes can be four hundred miles wide, so migrating birds sometimes find them impossible to avoid. And yet these birds are not to be underestimated. We can learn from their tenacity and determination to face our storms with the same quiet courage.

Bibliography

"A Whimbrel Called Hope." U.S. Fish & Wildlife Service, January 24, 2017. https://www.fws.gov/sssp/whimbrels.html.

Cosier, Susan. "Hope (the Whimbrel) Returns." Audubon, April 10, 2012. https://www.audubon.org/news/hope-whimbrel-returns.

McClain, Joseph. "Whimbrels Migrate Thousands of Miles, Only to be Gunned Down." LiveScience, October 5, 2011. https://www.livescience.com/16403-tracking-whimbrel-migration.html.

Photograph by Fiona Halliday

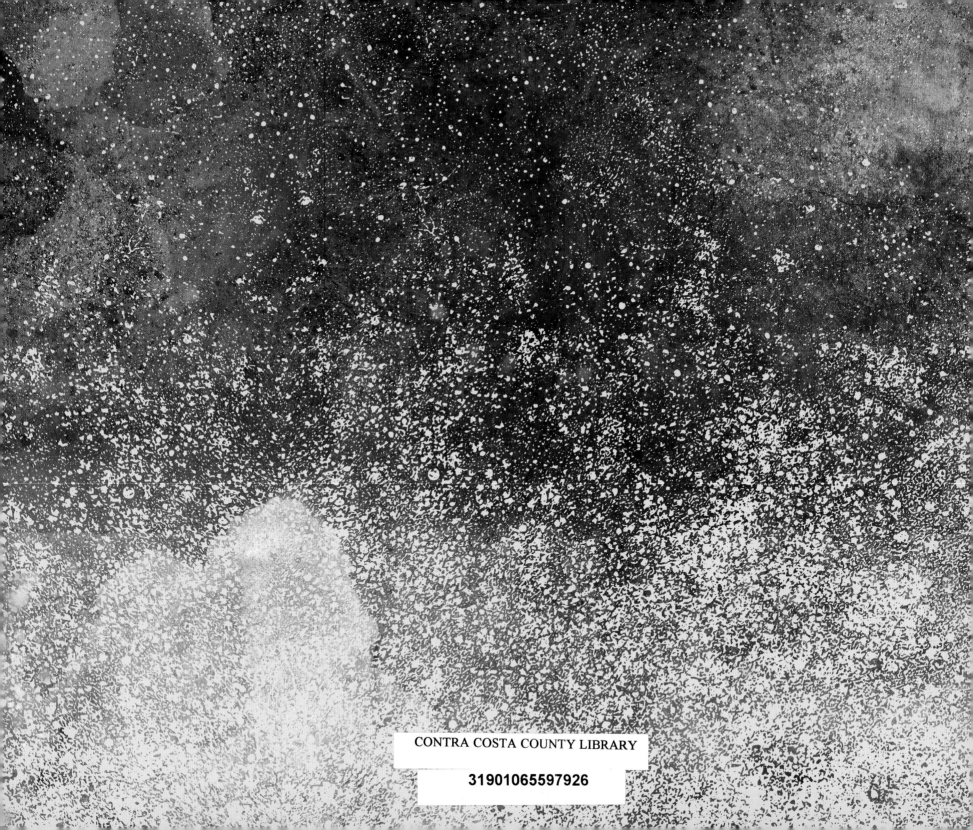